the MONSTER
at the end of this book

By Jon Stone

Illustrated by Michael Smollin

A GOLDEN BOOK · NEW YORK

Copyright © 1971 by Sesame Workshop. Copyright renewed 1999 by Sesame Workshop. All rights reserved.
Published in the United States by Golden Books, an imprint of Random House Children's Books, a division of
Random House, Inc., New York, in conjunction with Sesame Workshop. Sesame Street, Sesame Workshop, and
their logos are trademarks and service marks of Sesame Workshop. GOLDEN BOOKS, A GOLDEN BOOK, A LITTLE
GOLDEN BOOK, the G colophon, and the distinctive gold spine are registered trademarks of Random House, Inc.
Originally published in 1971 by Golden Books.

www.goldenbooks.com
www.randomhouse.com/kids
Educators and librarians, for a variety of teaching tools, visit us at www.randomhouse.com/teachers
Library of Congress Control Number: 2002112774
ISBN: 978-0-307-01085-8
Printed in the United States of America
40 39 38 37 36 35

This is
a very dull page.
What is on the
next page?

Maybe you do not understand. You see, turning pages will bring us to the end of this book, and there is a **Monster** at the end of this book...

...but **this** will stop you from turning pages. See? I am tying the pages together so you cannot....

THERE! I, Grover, am nailing this page to the next one so that you will not be able to turn it, and we will not get any closer to the Monster at the end of this book.

LL RIGHT!!
ALL RIGHT!!
ALL RIGHT!!

Do you know that every time you turn another page... you not only get us closer to the MONSTER at the end of this book, but you make a terrible mess.!

THE END
I told you and told you there was nothing to be afraid of.